'Sparkling with magi...
adventures *Grace-E*...

...otally bewitche...'

'Bubbling with magic, bravery and friendship this
is a charming read. *Grace-Ella: Witch Camp* will
cast a spell over you with its enchanting
and captivating storytelling.'

BookloverJo

'*Grace-Ella: Witch Camp* shimmers with magic,
friendship and adventure. Young readers will be totally
captivated by the adorable Grace-Ella, her witchy
friends and their furry feline companions.
A magnifulous-splendifulous book.'

Julie Sykes

Also in the series:

Grace-Ella: Spells for Beginners **(9781910080429)**

'A lively helping of fun, magic, friendship
and being true to yourself.'

Andrea Reece, Lovereading4Kids

To Bleddyn

Tomi, Ned and Cai

Always

Grace-Ella

WITCH CAMP

Sharon Marie Jones

Illustrated by
Adriana J Puglisi

Firefly

First published in 2019 by Firefly Press
25 Gabalfa Road, Llandaff North, Cardiff, CF14 2JJ
www.fireflypress.co.uk

A CIP catalogue record of this book
is available from the British Library.

ISBN 9781913102067
ebook ISBN 9781913102074

This book has been published with the support
of the Welsh Books Council.

Typeset by Claire Brisley.

Printed and bound by: Pulsio Sarl

Contents

Chapter One
The Letter

It was Saturday evening and Grace-Ella was pottering with her potions in the summer house at the bottom of the garden of number 32, Tŷ Mynydd Close.

'I wish the letter for Witch Camp would arrive,' she said, flopping down next to Mr Whiskins. 'It feels like I've been waiting forever. Do you think it's been lost in the post?'

A tap on the glass door interrupted her. Grace-Ella saw a very familiar silhouette, wearing a fur-trimmed deerstalker hat. Bedwyr!

Bedwyr lived next door and was bonkers about bugs. He collected and studied them in his garden shed, otherwise known as his 'Bug Lab'.

Bedwyr and Grace-Ella's other best friend, Fflur, were the only people, other than her parents, who knew Grace-Ella was a witch. She had found out when she was nine years, nine months and nine days old. Mr Whiskins had moved in and the Witch Council had sent her her must-have witch items: The Book of Rules, a Witch Tablet with her first spells and potions, a magic wand and a cauldron.

Grace-Ella had been scared to tell Bedwyr and Fflur the truth, in case they didn't want to stay friends with her, but now she loved that she could talk to them about her magic, with no secrets.

'What you up to?' Bedwyr asked, as he came in, dressed toe-to-top in his bug-busting gear.

'I've just finished bottling up my Fizzing

Firecracker potion ready for Bonfire Night. It'll explode across the night sky with colourful, fizzy sparks and loud bangs.'

'Booming brilliant,' said Bedwyr. 'I came over to see if you've had your letter about Witch Camp yet?'

'No,' sighed Grace-Ella. 'I was sure they'd hold it next week because it's the holidays. Maybe the Witch Council has decided that I'm not ready after all.'

'Do you want to go on a bug hunt to cheer you up?' asked Bedwyr. 'Next on my list is the assassin bug. They're beastly hunters that suck blood from their victims.'

'Gross,' said Grace-Ella, as they headed out into the garden. Mr Whiskins padded behind, always happy to be part of one of Bedwyr's hunts.

'I'll just get my torch,' said Bedwyr,

rummaging in his backpack. 'Dung beetles, I must have left it in my lab.' He looked up. 'But we can use Mr Whiskins … he seems to be glowing.'

Mr Whiskins was swatting his paw at something flickering fire-bright at the end of his snout.

Bedwyr snapped on his 'X-ray' swimming goggles and peered closer. 'It's a firefly.'

'It's a tickly fly,' said Mr Whiskins. 'It's making me want to snee … snee … ah pfft!'

The firefly flew into the air. With a swift swipe, Bedwyr caught the luminous bug in his butterfly net. The firefly fluttered angrily.

'I don't think it's very happy to be caught,' said Grace-Ella. 'It's looking rather annoyed.'

Freeing its trapped antennae from the net, the firefly floated into the sky. It hovered above their heads, before starting to spin, round and round, faster and faster, leaving a trail of fiery sparks in the air.

'What's it doing?' asked Grace-Ella.

Bedwyr had no idea what the bioluminescent bug was up to. 'Maybe it thinks it's in danger and is doing some kind of SOS call.'

The firefly flew even faster. It was burning so brightly, the air was warm on their faces. With a sudden crackle, the bright trail burst into flames. As it fizzled out, a shower of shimmering ashes fell to the ground. The firefly dipped low and blew on the ashes. Pumpkin-orange smoke billowed up into the sky.

'Bugtastic!' exclaimed Bedwyr.

'Witchtastic!' squealed Grace-Ella. 'Look!'

On the ground where the ashes had been was a golden envelope. The words 'Witch Camp' were written on it in bold, black letters. Grace-Ella picked it up in her trembling hands and hurried back inside the summer house.

She pulled out the letter and read it aloud.

Dear Grace-Ella,

I am pleased to inform you that you are ready for your very first Witch Camp. There, you can develop your magic spells and potions. If you do well, you will be awarded your Spells for Beginners certificate. Please arrive tomorrow, Sunday, no later than 3pm. Your parents must collect you at the same time next Friday.

A map of the camp and directions are enclosed, along with a list of items you'll need to bring with you. Please note that your parents must leave you and collect you at the Hollow Oak (see map).

I look forward to welcoming you.

Yours sincerely,

Penelope Pendle

(Head of the Witch Council)

'They haven't changed their minds about me after all,' grinned Grace-Ella.

She pulled two more folded sheets of paper out of the envelope: the map and the list. She spread the map out on her lap. Her eyes danced over the page as she tried to take it all in.

At the end of the winding road to the camp stood the Hollow Oak, just beyond the Old Stone Archway. The wooden cabins where they would be sleeping were in the Glade, the other side of Fir Tree Forest. Beyond the Glade were Whispering Willow Woods, home to the bubbling Belching Bog. The menacing Black Mountains towered high above the camp.

'It looks so magical,' whispered Grace-Ella.

'Well, it is Witch Camp,' answered Mr

Whiskins, very matter-of-factly.

'No need to be such a clever cat.'

'I can't help it if I've been given the gift of catty-cleverness.' Mr Whiskins arched his back proudly.

'Well then, I hope I've been given the gift of witchy-wisdom.' She sighed. 'I don't want to be a failure at camp. I bet the other witches will be much better than I am at spells and potions.'

'Stop being such a worry-wart,' said Mr Whiskins. 'You have magicked through your first spells with hardly a hiccup. You're a magnifulous-splendifulous witch.'

'Mr Whiskins is right,' added Bedwyr. 'You're the best witch I know.'

'I'm the only witch you know,' laughed Grace-Ella.

On the back of the map were the

directions. Once her parents had driven her under the Old Stone Archway to the Hollow Oak, Grace-Ella and Mr Whiskins should follow the Toadstool Trail through Fir Tree Forest until they arrived at the Glade.

'I hope we find it,' she said. 'I'm not very good at following trails. Last time we did orienteering with school, Fflur and I got completely lost because I was holding the compass upside down. We might not even get to Witch Camp.'

'I have an excellent sense of direction,' said Mr Whiskins. 'You'll be in safe paws with me.'

Next, Grace-Ella read out the list of things she would need to take with her.

Essential Items for Witch Camp

* *Sleeping bag*

* *Warm clothes and raincoat*

* *Suitable footwear (for woodland walking and forest foraging)*

* *Towel and toiletries*

* *Notebook and pen*

* *Witch Tablet*

* *Book of Rules*

* *Magic wand*

* *Cauldron*

* *Black cat*

'Well, that's charming,' said Mr Whiskins in disgust. 'Being listed as an item. How rude.'

'Don't worry, I won't be stuffing you into my rucksack,' said Grace-Ella. 'If it makes you feel better, you're definitely the most important item on my list.'

If cats had eyebrows, Mr Whiskins would certainly have raised his at that.

'I wish I could go with you,' said Bedwyr. 'Imagine how many bugs there'll be in camp. And magical ones too, just like that firefly. Witches have all the best fun.'

'It's going to be wicked,' said Grace-Ella. 'I'd better go and tell Mam and Dad and pack my things. I can't believe it! I'm actually going to Witch Camp!'

Chapter Two
Whoosh-and-Away to Witch Camp

Sunday started with Grace-Ella's bedroom curtains being whipped open in the middle of the pitch-dark night.

'Wakey-wakey, Grace-Ella. Bright and brisk is the Bev-an's motto,' her mam bellowed. Her mother always said Bev-an rather than Bevin, she thought it sounded better.

Grace-Ella disappeared under her duvet and groaned. Mrs Bevin had a ferocious fear of being late. She made sure that she arrived at least an hour early wherever she went, even if it was to drag Grace-Ella to the dentist.

With a sigh and a stretch, Grace-Ella promised herself that one day she would concoct a potion that would cure her mam of her being-late-a-phobia.

Sea mist drifted sleepily over Aberbetws as the Bevins set off. The car weaved along the winding coastal road, leaving behind the early morning squalling of seagulls.

Grace-Ella, now wide awake, chattered excitedly. 'It's going to be the best week ever. I bet we'll cook on a campfire and learn awesome spells and dangerous potions and even fly on a broomstick.'

'Don't you need a flying licence for that?'

said Mrs Bevin. 'And it's not exactly the best time of year for camping. You'd think they'd put a bit more planning into it. After all this miserable weather, it's going to be horribly sludgy and muddy. Don't you agree, Selwyn?'

Mr Bevin shrugged.

Mrs Bevin sighed in that way of hers. 'Well, if you end up catching pneumonia or dropping from the sky, I shall make an official complaint.'

After what seemed like an endless bumping along a single-track country lane, Mr Bevin pulled into a passing place to study the directions.

'Are you sure we're going the right way?' asked Mrs Bevin.

'According to the map, we should see the Old Stone Archway in a couple of miles,' said Mr Bevin.

True to his word, exactly two miles ahead, an old stone archway loomed into view. Mr Bevin drove through and stopped the car.

To their left stood what could only be the Hollow Oak. Its barren branches stretched up like skeletal arms. Its roots sprawled above the ground like long, gnarled fingers. There was a large hollow at the base of its thick trunk. A lone blackbird perched silently on one of the branches.

'It's dreadfully quiet. I'm really not sure about abandoning you here,' said Mrs Bevin.

'You're not abandoning me. This is the exact spot where the directions say to leave me. Mr Whiskins is with me and the other witches will be just the other side of the forest.'

Grace-Ella leapt out of the car, hoisted

her rucksack onto her back and clutched her cauldron.

'Make sure you brush your teeth every night and wear your coat and hat,' fussed her mam.

'We'll be looking forward to hearing all about your witchy adventures next weekend,' her dad added.

Grace-Ella waved until the car disappeared. 'Right, then. Where do you think we should start?' she asked Mr Whiskins. 'If we're meant to follow the Toadstool Trail, I suppose we need to look for toadstools.'

And right there, at the foot of the Hollow Oak, was a cluster of scarlet toadstools.

'Then I guess we start right here, inside the tree,' said Mr Whiskins. He leapt inside the hollow trunk.

'Inside the tree?' said Grace-Ella.

She stepped closer and peered in. It was gloomy and smelt damp and earthy. 'There's nothing in here. I think we should try to find a path. There must be one that leads into the forest.'

'Wait a whisker,' echoed Mr Whiskins' voice. 'I do believe that my cat's eyes can see a door.'

'A door? You don't get doors in trees,' said Grace-Ella.

But as right as right is not left, on the opposite side of the Hollow Oak's trunk was a door. Mr Whiskins pushed it open and sprang through. Grace-Ella followed. Scrambling over slippery moss-covered roots, she found herself on a path leading right into Fir Tree Forest.

'That's impossible! The tree was at the side of the road. How can it have moved to the edge of the forest?'

'We're entering the world of witches,' said Mr Whiskins. 'There will be all sorts of strange goings-on this week.'

This made Grace-Ella tingle from the tips of her toes to the very tip of her nose.

They followed the sun-striped path through the forest. The carpet of russet and gold leaves scrunched underfoot. Twigs cracked

like a bonfire when they stepped on them and the air smelt autumn-fresh.

'Do you think I'll have to do any tests in camp?' Grace-Ella pondered. 'I'm rubbish at tests. I get all collywobbly and my brain goes blank.'

'You're as bright as a sprite,' said Mr Whiskins. 'Born to be a witch.'

She couldn't disagree with that fact, so Grace-Ella tried to push her wobbly worries aside.

When it was beginning to feel like they had been walking for miles, the path forked into two.

'Now what do we do?' said Grace-Ella. 'How do we know which path we should follow?'

'There must be some toadstools that'll tell us,' replied Mr Whiskins.

'This toadstool won't tell you which is the

right way, but myself here will help you …
or lead you astray,' trilled a little voice.

Grace-Ella looked around to see who
had spoken.

An enormous toadstool stood partly
hidden in the undergrowth. Sitting on
its top was a small enchanting creature
dressed in green. He had pointy ears, a
snub nose and a very mischievous grin.

'You … you're … are you a real forest
pixie?' asked Grace-Ella.

'Oh great, a prankster pixie, that's all we
need,' groaned Mr Whiskins.

'I am indeed a forest pixie. Buddy
Whiffleflip,' said the pixie, jumping down
from his toadstool and giving a regal bow.
'Charmed to meet you.'

'It's nice to meet you too, Buddy
Whiffleflip,' said Grace-Ella.

'So,' said Buddy, 'here the trail ends

as it forks into two,
the right path to follow
is now up to you.
You must solve my riddle
of the Toadstool Trail,
be wise and bright witches
or else you'll fail.'
Grace-Ella's stomach did a flippety-flip.

She knew she wasn't going to be able to solve the riddle. They were never going to find their way into Witch Camp.

Buddy Whiffleflip unrolled a paper scroll from his pocket and cleared his throat.

'*Now carefully listen*
to this tiny scamp
and un-riddle my words
to get into camp:
Lizard's leg and a pumpkin whole,
Eye of a rat and the tail of a mole,
Frog's toe in and the claws of a shrew,
'Tis ready now to bubble and brew.
Which is the way you'll choose to go?
Right or left? You should now know.'

'Bothersome bats,' mumbled Grace-Ella miserably. 'I don't know which way to choose. It made no sense at all.'

Mr Whiskins on the other hand grinned. 'Don't be so quick to give up! It's as clear as an open cat flap. You don't have to make sense of the words. You just need to use the first letter of the first word of each line to make a new word.'

Grace-Ella studied the words on the scroll. 'L, E, F, T. They spell left! Mr Whiskins, you are the cleverest cat in the whole of the cat kingdom. Goodbye, Buddy Whiffleflip. Thank you for your help.'

The little pixie hopped back onto his toadstool with a cheery jingle-jangle from the bell on his pointed hat.

Grace-Ella and Mr Whiskins headed down the left path. It didn't take long for the trees to open up and just ahead was the Glade.

As she edged closer, Grace-Ella was a jumble of nerves and excitement. She could see the busy witch teachers dressed in long black cloaks. A campfire was burning low in the centre. Sitting on a fallen tree trunk was a girl fidgeting with the suitcase at her feet. Next to her dozed a very wiry black cat.

Taking a deep breath, Grace-Ella headed into Witch Camp.

Chapter Three
Dibble and Dobbles

Grace-Ella stopped a few paces from the fire. A blackbird swooped down and landed on the ground in front of her. In a puff of purple smoke, the blackbird disappeared and standing in its place was Penelope Pendle, Head of the Witch Council.

'Congratulations on solving the riddle and following the Toadstool Trail correctly,' she said. 'There are some final preparations to be made, so I'll leave you two early birds to get to know each other. There are sure to be some young witches who'll fail and will need rescuing.'

Grace-Ella dropped her rucksack and sat down on the tree trunk. She glanced at the other girl, who was chewing her bottom lip.

'I'm Grace-Ella and this is Mr Whiskins.'

'I'm Dilys Dibble and this is Dobbles,' said the girl shyly.

Dilys was small with mousy-coloured hair. She kept scrunching up her nose to push up her glasses, which made her front teeth stick out.

'It's really exciting to be here, isn't it?' said Grace-Ella. 'I'm a bit nervous as well though.'

'I'm not excited,' said Dilys tearfully. 'I don't want to be here at all.'

'Oh! Don't you want your Spells for Beginners certificate? I'm going to have mine framed above my bed and have twinkly lights around it ... if I get it, that is.'

'I definitely won't get my certificate,' said Dilys. 'I'm a useless witch. My spells always go wrong and my potions cause nothing but stinky explosions. Mam-gu has completely given up on me. "Dilys," she says, "you are the worst witch that the Dibble family has ever had."'

'That sounds a bit harsh,' said Grace-Ella. 'You can't be that bad. You've already solved the riddle to get here.'

'That was a mistake,' Dilys sighed. 'I assumed the path to the right would be the right path because it's called the right path, so we followed the left path in the hope that we'd get lost and be sent back home.'

'Oh,' said Grace-Ella once again. 'Well, maybe being at Witch Camp will help you prove to yourself that you are a good witch. Even the best witches make mistakes. And the Witch Council thinks you're ready to be here, otherwise they wouldn't have sent you a letter.'

'I have no idea why I received a letter.
What kind of witch can't cast a simple spell?
Or prepare a potion that actually works? I'll
never be a proper witch. Not ever.'

Dilys wiped her eyes with a tissue and
blew her nose. The thunderous sound woke
Dobbles, who fell off the tree trunk with
a meow. He clawed his way back up and
curled into a quivering ball on Dilys's lap.

'Is he all right?' asked Grace-Ella.

'He's frightened of loud noises,' explained

Dilys, 'and heights … and the dark…'

'Old Dobbles sounds like a right owly-hoot,' muttered Mr Whiskins.

Grace-Ella gave her cat a narrow-eyed warning. 'Mr Whiskins will look out for Dobbles this week, won't you?'

'Always ready to help a cat in distress,' replied Mr Whiskins, not looking pleased.

'And we can look out for each other too,' added Grace-Ella.

'You won't want any help from me,' said Dilys shaking her head. 'I'll only be a nuisance. Do you know, the worst thing is that Mam and Dad were so proud when I was born. They named me Dilys because it means "genuine and true". They said, little Dilys will be a genuine and true witch, the best kind there is.'

'There you are then. Your mam and dad

are proud of you even if your mam-gu isn't,' said Grace-Ella.

'Mam and Dad are devastated I'm so bad. They've bought hundreds of books about magic and spells and potions. They have their noses stuck in them every evening. You have to walk sideways like a crab to get through the walls of books in the hallway. Aunty Carol was jealous that none of her children had any magic, but now she's super-smug. "Such a shame," she always says when she visits, "that Dilys is so dreadful at being a witch."'

Grace-Ella didn't know what to say. She knew what it was like to be not very good at something. She could never get her schoolwork right on her first attempt and always seemed to be the last to finish in class. She hoped she would be able to help

Dilys during the week ahead.

Before long, the camp was buzzing with young witches and their black cats. Once the last witch had arrived safely (after being found wandering halfway up the Black Mountains), Penelope Pendle began the introduction.

'Welcome to your first Witch Camp. I hope you'll all have a wonderful week developing your witch skills. Firstly, you'll be divided into groups of four and allocated to a cabin. You'll find a timetable on the back of your cabin door telling you which activity you'll be doing each day. At the end of each activity, you'll have time to complete a test on your Witch Tablet. Each test will allow you to win gold stars. The number of stars you collect will determine whether or not you receive your Spells for Beginners certificate.'

Grace-Ella's shoulders stooped. She never did well in her school tests. If only she had studied before coming to camp. But she'd been having far too much fun with her spells and potions to sit learning revision notes. Maybe she and Dilys would be able to help each other, if they were put in the same cabin. She crossed her fingers and tried her best to cross her toes as Penelope Pendle began dividing them into their groups.

She tapped the rim of a large black cauldron four times with her magic wand and said, 'Witches, hold out your starry hand, then wait to see where the fireflies land.'

One of the signs of being a witch was that they each had a green star on the palm of their left hand. Out of the cauldron flew four fluttering fireflies. They landed on the starry palms of four witches. They were the first group.

Tap tap tap tap…

Another four fireflies flew into the air. The first landed on Grace-Ella's hand. Her breath whooshed out of her with relief, like a popped balloon, as another landed on Dilys's. She looked around to see who the other two girls in their group were.

One was very tall with long curly red hair and a peppering of freckles on her nose. The other had shiny black hair and was busily jotting something in her notebook. They shyly grouped together and introduced themselves. Mati Meredith was the girl with the red hair and her black cat was called Moonbeam. The other girl was Aisha Patel and her cat Twilight.

After everyone had been split into groups, the four girls headed off to find their cabin, led by the fireflies. The four cats followed, circling each other, trying to decide who was going to be Top Cat in the

cabin. It probably wouldn't be poor Dobbles, who kept leaping in fright when he caught sight of his own tail.

Mati unlocked their cabin door. 'My fellow witches,' she said, 'let's enter our coven.'

Chapter Four
'Broken Rules Breed Folly and Fools'

The four fireflies floated into glass jars hanging from wooden beams, casting a golden glow around the cabin. There were two bunkbeds with two cat beds at the foot of each. Four black cloaks hung on pegs, ready for their Leaving Ceremony on Friday.

'I'll have this bed if that's OK?' said Mati, climbing onto one of the top bunks.

Aisha happily sat on the bottom, which left the other bunk for Grace-Ella and Dilys.

'Right,' said Mati, 'let's get straight to work. Every coven has a Head Witch. Who wants to be ours? I'll be it, if nobody else wants to. Aunty Lilith always tells me that I've been born to lead. Is that all right with you? Or we could have a vote, if you prefer?'

Beaming at the other three girls, she carried on. 'This week is going to be brilliant. We should have a name for our coven, shouldn't we? How about the Daring Dragons? Or the Midnight Roses? Roses are beautiful but thorny. That's absolutely perfect, don't you think? We are the Midnight Roses. We're going to be the best coven that Witch Camp has ever had.'

Mati gabbled uninterrupted about how they were going to be the star spellers and perfect potionists. Dilys paled and Aisha sat in stunned silence, her pen poised over her notebook and her chestnut-brown eyes unblinking. Grace-Ella suspected that Witch Camp was going to be anything but dull with Mati leading them.

Having settled in, all the young witches headed back to the campfire for a supper of cheesy-topped, fire-baked potatoes and sugar-and-spice donuts.

'Did you know that fireflies aren't actually flies?' said Aisha, watching the glowing bugs dancing in the sky. 'They're beetles.'

'Really?' said Mati. 'Well, you'd think that the bug scientists could have come up with a better name for them, like burning beetles or something.'

'In some places they're called lightning bugs or moon bugs,' continued Aisha. 'Where my dad grew up in India, they call them minna-minni, which is my favourite name for them.'

'Wow,' said Grace-Ella. 'You know a lot about fireflies. My friend, Bedwyr, is obsessed with bugs. He wants to be a bugologist when he's older. You'd get on so well with him.'

Aisha blushed. 'I just like to read interesting facts, and store them away in my brain. Dad says I'm like a squirrel squirrelling away acorns.'

'I think that's amazing,' said Mati, munching on her donut. 'I'm more practical than factual. Everyone has a special talent, that's what Aunty Lilith says, and I bet our talents will blend brilliantly. So who do you think will be our toughest competition?'

'Competition for what?' asked Grace-Ella.

'For being the best coven. I heard there'll be extra stars given for good witch work, not just for doing well in the tests, and then our stars will be added together at the end of the week for the Best Coven prize. Cabin Six look like they're already hatching, don't they?'

Grace-Ella, relieved to learn that she could win stars for being a good witch, not just a clever witch, glanced at the group of witches from Cabin Six. She was half expecting to see them nestling on eggs.

'I bet their brains are buzzing, planning and plotting for the week ahead,' continued Mati. 'We'll have to make sure that we're one step ahead at all times.'

Their conversation ended as Penelope
Pendle stood up.

'It's almost time to return to your cabins,
so some final words from me. You're here
this week to learn and develop and of
course to have fun and enjoy yourselves.
But there are rules that must be followed.
Deliberately breaking a rule will have
you expelled and back on your doorstep
at home quicker than you can bellow,
"Broomsticks!"'

The young witches sat quietly. Nobody
wanted to be booted out of Witch Camp.

'I want you to memorise the wise motto
of our founding member, Aldyth Bedortha:
Broken rules breed folly and fools...'

Penelope Pendle paused, allowing the
witches to absorb these words as they

echoed in the cool evening air.

'Firstly, you must follow the timetable. There will be no skipping any activities. Cabin lights-out is at ten o'clock. You must not leave your cabin after lights-out, unless it's an emergency. Bickering will not be tolerated. And of course, you must always abide by the Nine Golden Rules, even whilst you're here at Witch Camp. So just in case you need reminding, listen carefully before you head off to bed...'

She opened The Book of Rules. Aldyth Bedortha's shrill voice read aloud the nine rules:

The Nine Golden Rules

Rule 1: Always cast your magic in private. Only in the company of other witches can spells be cast openly.

Rule 2: Never use your magic for revenge. Your magic is to be used for good only.

Rule 3: Never allow personal greed to affect your magic. Your magic cannot be used to make you rich.

Rule 4: Never use your magic to cheat. You must not cast spells to help you cheat in any circumstances. You must continue to learn life's skills and lessons in the same way as people with no magic.

Rule 5: Never use your magic on unsuspecting victims. A person should always be aware that magic is being cast on them.

Rule 6: Do not exceed nine spells on one person. A non-witch has a spell limit of nine. Exceeding nine spells will result in permanent changes to that person.

Rule 7: Never cast a spell on another witch. Casting a spell on another witch tampers greatly with her powers and can be extremely dangerous.

Rule 8: Always follow spells and potions carefully. Do not attempt to alter an established spell or potion – the results could be disastrous.

Rule 9: Report mistakes immediately. If you cast a wrong spell, or a spell doesn't work as it should, you must report the incident to the Witch Council, who will then manage the situation.

Back in the cabin, the girls rummaged through their suitcases and rucksacks to find their pyjamas and toothbrushes. All four cats happily hopped into their cat beds, stretched, gave four almighty cat yawns and curled up for a good night's catnap.

Aisha read from the timetable on the back of the door. 'Breakfast is at eight o'clock and our activity tomorrow is Forest Foraging with Witch Hazel.'

'Brilliant,' said Mati, wriggling into her sleeping bag. 'I bet we'll learn about magical plants that can do really weird stuff, even dangerous ones that can probably poison us. Didn't I say this was going to be a brilliant week? Let's get straight to sleep so that we're the first ones up in the morning. That will probably give us bonus stars.'

As night fell almost silent around the cabin (Dobbles had a rather annoying whimpery snore), Grace-Ella flipped and fiddled and flopped and flumped. She was far too excited to sleep. She was actually at Witch Camp! She couldn't wait for all the activities and she already liked her three new friends. Although Mati talked a lot, she wasn't a bully like Amelia back at school. She simply seemed to be so full of words that she couldn't stop them from flowing out, just like a burst dam.

Grace-Ella shuffled to the end of her bunk, hoping that Mr Whiskins would be as wide-awake as she was. But he was fast asleep, a curled-up furry ball with twitchy whiskers. She hung topsy-turvy over the side to see if Dilys wanted to witch-chat. But she too was fast asleep, snug as a snail with Dobbles in her sleeping bag.

Grace-Ella crawled back up the bed and picked up her copy of The Book of Rules. Reading usually helped her to feel sleepy at home. Her firefly fluttered out of its jar and landed on her pillow. Its glowing body illuminated the words so that she could read them in the dark.

She quickly skipped the page of the Nine Golden Rules. She didn't want Aldyth Bedortha to wake the others up.

The rest of the book was filled with stories of witches who had broken rules, starting in the seventeenth century and going all the way to the seventeenth of last month. This puzzled Grace-Ella. How could a book she'd been given months ago, when she became a witch, include a story from only a couple of weeks ago? Well, it is a magic book, she imagined Mr Whiskins saying.

As if to prove this point, the pages began to flutter and flick over. Grace-Ella waited until the book finally stilled. She began to read the story it had chosen for her...

Chapter Five
Bella Bwt

The Curse of the Clucky Chickens

Bella Bwt was born on the second of May, 1657. She lived with her parents in a ramshackle cottage where rainwater tinkled into tin buckets through holes in the roof. Her father farmed for Sir Talbot for ten pennies a week and the rotten roof over their heads. They survived mainly on bread and broth.

Bella didn't go to school. She spent her days in the forest.

Life changed for the Bwts when Sir Talbot died and his son Cadog took over the land. Cadog Talbot was a miser. He had twin sons, Twm and Wil. The twins would come rampaging through the forest, whooping and howling, hunting Bella down like a wild animal.

When Bella was nine years old, a black cat turned up at their cottage. The black cat revealed that she was a witch and gave her The Book of Rules, a spell-book, her magic wand and her cauldron. The Bwts knew they had to keep this a secret. At that time, people believed that witches were dangerous, and they could be hanged or thrown into a river to drown. Bella's parents knew she was a good witch and would do no harm to anyone.

Not long after, Bella's mother became very ill. With her black cat at her side, Bella roamed the forest searching for medicinal plants. She worked long into the moonlit

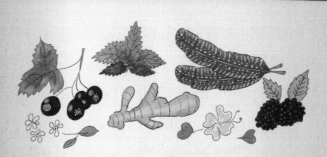

nights, concocting a potion that could make her mother better. After several tries, she finally knew what she needed. She collected black bryony berries, white yarrow flowers, wild peppermint and ginger. The final ingredient she needed was chicken feathers.

Late at night, she crept into the Talbots' farmyard and swiped one of the sleeping chickens from its coop. But Twm and Wil were watching from their bedroom window. Finally, they had proof. The girl was a thief and their father would have to throw the Bwts off their land.

Bella finished her potion and made her mother drink it. As her mother's raging fever began to drop, Cadog Talbot rode up to the cottage. He called Bella a thief and threatened her parents that he would tell the magistrate. Bella would be put in the stocks on the village square and whipped.

Bella told him that she had only plucked some feathers from the chicken and had returned it safely to the farm. She explained that she needed them for the medicine to make her mother better. This angered Cadog Talbot even more. She was a witch! He said if they didn't all leave immediately, the magistrate could have her killed.

Bella was furious. While her mother and father gathered their few belongings, she snuck back to the Talbots' farm and shimmied up the drainpipe to the twins' bedroom. Swirling her wand, she whispered her magic words.

'Scratch and peck will the Talbot boys,
Flapping and squawking, such terrible noise.
Rotten and stinky eggs they'll lay,
As crazy cluckers they'll forever stay.'

Bella and her parents travelled for a long time. They stumbled across a derelict hut in the woods and made it their new home.

One evening, a stranger came to their door. Her name was Agnes Waterhouse and she was a member of the Witch Council. She told the Bwts how, after they'd left, the Talbot twins had turned into chickens. She explained that Bella had broken rule number two of the Nine Golden Rules: "*Never use your magic for revenge*".

Bella was distraught. She had no idea that she had broken any rules because she couldn't read. She had never been to school and had never learnt her letters. Her mother sobbed and begged. Agnes Waterhouse explained that the Nine Golden Rules couldn't be broken, or they would have witches wreaking havoc across the country.

But Agnes could see that Bella was a very gifted young witch. She didn't want to take her magic from her. Her punishment was to live as a chicken for a whole year. With a swish of Agnes's wand, Bella was pecking about on the hut floor.

Nobody knows for sure what happened to Bella Bwt after that. Some say a fox caught her. Others say she laid the largest, tastiest eggs every morning and that after her punishment was up, the Bwts went to live in peace high up in the mountains.

Grace-Ella's eyes were heavy as she closed the book. Poor Bella, she thought. She didn't deserve to be punished. It wasn't her fault she couldn't read. She couldn't possibly have known about the Nine Golden Rules. She hoped that Bella had survived and had lived happily in the mountains.

With a sleepy sigh, she finally drifted off.

Chapter Six
Forest Foraging

'No dawdling,' shouted Witch Hazel as they set off foraging the following morning. Witch Hazel was a very tall witch, who walked briskly with a giraffe stride. 'Make sure you stay on the path. I don't want to be wasting time trying to find anyone who gets lost.'

The young witches and their cats followed along the path through Fir Tree Forest. They carried their cauldrons filled with empty potion bottles, foraging tools and their notebooks and pens. Mr Whiskins had Dobbles on his tail from the moment they pounced off.

'Today I'll be showing you how to forage

some very useful plants for your potions,' explained Witch Hazel. 'I will also be teaching you about the ones to avoid. There are some very poisonous plants out here and unless you want to end up d-e-a-d you need to learn how to identify them.'

Dilys gave Grace-Ella a nervous nudge. 'Wh-what did she mean?'

'Don't worry. I'm sure she's just saying it to make sure that we listen and behave. She's not really going to let anyone die, is she?'

Witch Hazel came to a halt and the young witches gathered around her.

'The first thing I want to show you is dragon's dew. Dragon's dew can only be found on a lace-weaver spider's web, which you'll see spun onto the tree next to me.'

Pretty patterned gossamer webs hung woven between the branches. Dewdrops glistened on them like rainbow teardrops.

'You'll need your pipettes to suck up the dew. Remember to label your bottles as we go along and write down anything useful you notice in your notebooks.'

The witches set about collecting drops of dragon's dew.

'The web's silk is a pale blue colour,' said Aisha, writing this in her notebook. 'Apparently ancient potionists believed that dragon's dew could turn even the ugliest thing into something beautiful.'

Grace-Ella wished she was as clever as Aisha. Her notebook was set out in alphabetical order, with sub-titles and underlined words. She was sure to pass her tests and collect all her gold stars. Grace-Ella, on the other hand, felt like a simmering stewpot of facts and figures that

were spilling splish-sploshedly onto her notebook pages.

'On we go,' shouted Witch Hazel, clicking her fingers.

They foraged leaves and flowers, herbs and berries, pine cones and pine needles. Grace-Ella couldn't wait to start practising with their forest ingredients. There were so many strange-sounding plants that she had never heard of — hairy bittercress, shepherd's purse, fat hen — how was she ever going to remember them all?

'Now look very carefully at this,' said Witch Hazel, as they stopped once again. The leafy plant she was pointing at had purple bell-shaped flowers, with a shiny black berry in the centre. 'This is deadly nightshade. Notice its rich purple colour and sweet berry fragrance, which will grow stronger the longer we stand next to it.'

The air around them was scented with the sweetest smell Grace-Ella had ever known. Her mouth watered. All the young witches shuffled closer, hypnotised by its deliciousness. As one of the witches slowly reached out her hand to pluck one of the berries, Witch Hazel clicked her fingers sharply, snapping them out of their dreamy daze.

'That is exactly what this plant does,' she warned. 'It draws you in until you can't resist picking a berry and popping it into your mouth. Jazmin, if I hadn't stopped you just now, you would have devoured that berry without batting an eye. But the deadly nightshade's berries are bursting with poison. Just one would be enough to unbalance your brain. A handful, and you could end up d-e-a-d.'

Jazmin leapt away from the poisonous plant as if a bolt of electricity had shot through her.

'There have been cases where witches have used this plant to cause harm to others,' warned Witch Hazel. 'As we all know, having magic at our fingertips is a wonderful gift. But magic can be dangerous. It must be used correctly and

safely. This is why we have the Nine Golden Rules to abide by. On we go.'

The morning tick-tocked quickly by. They learnt how to snip the snapdragon flower before it snapped its spiky teeth into their hands. They tasted bark from the groaning toothache tree that tickled their tongues.

Witch Hazel proudly showed them the plant that she had been named after. It had long yellow spaghetti petals that wriggled through their fingers, and a spicy red fruit which popped off its stalk without warning. When the fruit took flight, they had to try to catch them in small nets before they splattered on the ground.

Mati risked a sneaky step off the path. She immediately became tangled in the creeping ivy lurking in the undergrowth. It wound itself around her ankles, trapping her. Mati tried her best to bat the ivy away. 'Get off me, you creepy creeper,' she shrieked.

Witch Hazel and her magic wand had to come to the rescue. She tapped the creeping ivy and it slunk back to hide.

'Remember that you're at Witch Camp,' she said sternly. 'The plants here don't behave in the same way as ordinary plants. The creeping ivy would have wrapped itself so tightly around your whole body that … well … let's not have me spell it out again.'

On through the forest they walked, no one daring to leave the path. With their scalpels, they scraped gooey witches' butter from rotten wood. They learnt not to pick hogweed as it would leave a nasty burn on their hands. By lunchtime, their potion bottles were filled and carefully labelled.

'I have one last plant to show you before

we head back to camp,' said Witch Hazel. 'It's the most magical plant of all, the one that every witch, since the beginning of time, wishes to have. This plant is like the pot of gold at the end of the rainbow or a cloud lined with silver. Would you like to see it?'

The bug-eyed witches nodded.

'Then follow me.'

Chapter Seven
The Stinging Screamer

Witch Hazel led the way deep into Fir
Tree Forest. The shadows darkened and
the air felt goose-bumply cold. Grace-Ella
shivered. She wouldn't want to be out here
on her own in the middle of the night.

Mr Whiskins pranced playfully, dodging
in front of her on the path, and Grace-Ella
felt a little bit braver. Dobbles was hiding
in Dilys's cauldron. Moonbeam, who was
as brave and bold as Mati, was strutting
ahead. Twilight, a very clever and cautious
cat, trotted close to Aisha.

'You will only find this special plant
hiding in the dark belly of a magical forest,'
explained Witch Hazel, stopping next to a
fallen tree.

She carefully crouched down and parted the dangly roots of the tree, as if she was opening the curtains of a theatre show. 'Peer behind the roots and you'll see it.'

The witches knelt down to catch their first glimpse of the magical plant.

'Look at its fuzzy cream flowers; each flower has five pointed petals,' explained Witch Hazel.

'Just like the five-pointed stars on our hand,' said Aisha, scribbling down this new fact.

'Precisely. Hundreds of years ago, when witches were thought of as wicked and dangerous, our ancestors buried their spell books in magical forests around the world. Where a spell book is buried, this magical plant grows.'

'Do we have to dig up the plant to find the spell book?' asked Mati.

'No, no. The spell books have long ago decomposed and become part of the earth. But each one of the flowers knows one of the ancient spells. Once it whispers its secret spell, the flower will wither and die. You must take very good care of the plant, to make sure that it continues to bloom new flowers. If the plant dies, then all the ancient spells it knows will be lost forever.'

'Does it have a name?' asked one of the witches.

Witch Hazel said, 'Its name is … the stinging screamer.'

'I don't like the sound of this plant anymore,' whispered Dilys. 'It doesn't sound very friendly.'

'Why is it called the stinging screamer?' asked Aisha, eager to learn as much as she could and fill up her notebook before returning to camp.

'If you try to pick it before your magic is strong enough, when you pull on its stalk, its flowers will begin to scream,' explained Witch Hazel. 'The longer and harder you pull, the more terrifying the screaming will become. Eventually the little hairs on the stalk will shoot a sharp sting up your arm, forcing you to let it go. This is to make sure that it never ends up in the wrong hands. The stinging screamer will only let itself be chosen by those it knows will use its magic wisely. Many witches take years to be able to successfully forage the stinging screamer. Some never manage it.'

'Do we get to have a go today?' asked Mati.

'As I said, it can take years to learn how to harness the magic needed to pull up the stinging screamer,' said Witch Hazel.

'Oh … but maybe we could have a little try … just to see,' said Mati, reaching out her hand.

'You've only just been given your magic powers. You're not ready to…'

It was too late. Mati couldn't contain her excitement. She was too tantalisingly close to the magical plant. She wrapped her hands around the stinging screamer's stalk and began to pull.

Spine-tingling, ear-splitting screaming filled the forest. Birds burst from the trees in fright. Some girls screamed too, whilst others held their hands over their ears.

'Please come out of the ground,' yelled Mati as she yanked the plant. 'I'm the best witch owner you'll ever have. Oh, please come out, please…'

The more she begged, the louder the

flowers screamed, their petals opened wide. In the middle of each flower there were two long filaments with sticky pink tips that quivered like tickly tonsils.

The other witches watched in frozen horror. With a cry, Mati suddenly flew back as a sharp sting shot up her arm. She sat dazed on the ground, empty-handed.

'I tried to warn you,' said Witch Hazel.
'You're not ready.'

Mati looked red-faced. 'I would have
taken care of it. Aunty Lilith says that I'm
more than ready for advanced spells.'

'One step at a time, Mati. You can't
force your magic, just as you can't fly a
broomstick without first having a broom.'

'So we have to wait until we're old and
wrinkly before we can forage one,' Mati
mumbled sulkily.

'Not at all. You just need to learn how to
harness your magic and not be quite so …
impatient. The plant will know when it has
found a trusted owner. Now I think we'll
leave the stinging screamer in peace and
head back to camp. You can finish writing
up notes on your newly foraged plants and
complete your Foraging Test.'

With their ears still ringing from the screaming, the witches gladly followed Witch Hazel back to the quiet of the Glade.

'I definitely would have pulled up the stinging screamer if I'd had more time,' pouted Mati as she started up her Witch Tablet. 'I was rushing because everyone wanted to get back to camp and it must have thought I wouldn't have time to look after it properly. As soon as I get home I'm going to ask Aunty Lilith to take me to a magical forest so that I can collect one. I'll probably become the youngest witch ever to own one and win a special award.'

They all opened up their Foraging Test on their tablets. Grace-Ella nervously suggested that they work together because she knew both she and Dilys were very worried about failing the test. Mati and Aisha readily agreed, but once they started, they realised they had each been given different questions and so they had to work by themselves.

For every question they got correct, a gold star dropped into a cauldron at the bottom of the screen. Each test was timed. Once the glittery green sand had emptied from the egg timer on the top left of the screen, a lid closed on the cauldron and no more stars could be won.

Grace-Ella wished that Mr Whiskins was there to help her, but the witch cats were being treated to some paw pampering and a moggy massage with Witch Catkins.

She tried her very best to answer all the questions before her cauldron closed. She didn't have time to read through her muddled notes, so she hoped she could remember as much as possible to win enough stars. She felt sickly in her tummy when she thought about not getting her certificate. She didn't want to disappoint her mam and dad. She was determined to show them that she was good at being a witch and make them proud.

Chapter Eight
Dream Dust

In the middle of the night, Grace-Ella was woken up by a shuffling sound in the cabin. With heavy-lidded eyes, she peered over the edge of her bunk. In the golden glow from the fireflies, she could see Dilys sitting cross-legged on the floor. Her potion bottles were lined up in front of her and she was drawing very carefully on her labels.

Grace-Ella rubbed her sleepy eyes. Hadn't Dilys labelled her bottles when they were in the forest? She was about to ask her if everything was OK, but something stopped her. The way Dilys was labelling her potion bottles secretly in the middle of the night made Grace-Ella think that she didn't want to be disturbed.

She snuggled back down in her sleeping bag, but her brain wouldn't stop whirling. Earlier that evening, the four of them had compared how many gold stars they'd won at the end of their Foraging Test. Mati had won twenty stars out of the possible twenty-five and complained that her tablet was faulty. Aisha had collected all twenty-five stars. Grace-Ella had won eighteen stars before being timed-out. Dilys had mumbled that she hadn't done very well. Aisha had reassured her that it was just the first test and that she'd have plenty of time to catch up.

Grace-Ella had a niggle in the back of her brain. It was like an itch that she couldn't quite reach. Perhaps she should talk to Mati and Aisha to see if they had noticed anything odd about Dilys's behaviour? But

then she didn't want Dilys to think they
were talking about her behind her back.
She decided to keep a closer eye on her new
friend, to make sure she was all right.

The next morning, the young witches set
up their cauldrons on long tables under
a large wooden gazebo, ready for their
Cauldron Class with Witch Buggins.

Witch Buggins was a remarkably small witch. Her black cloak swished along the ground as she bustled about the camp like a busy beetle. She was very rarely still, constantly collecting, mixing, pouring and bottling.

'Good morning, witches,' she said, hopping onto a wooden step so that she could see over the tables. 'Preparing a

potion is just like baking a cake. All you need are the correct ingredients, a wooden spoon and your magic spell. Mix it all up and bizzle-buzzle, your potion is ready. We're going to start with the Dream Dust potion. A sprinkling of Dream Dust on your pillow will send you to sleep to dream your dreamiest dreams. And who knows, maybe your dream will come true.'

'My dreamiest dream is that one day I'll be prime minister,' boomed Mati. 'I'll be the best prime minister the country has ever elected. My first rule will be to ban zoos because animals should be free in the wild, but I'll allow my best friends to have a special permit to keep one wild animal each, because imagine how cool it would be to gallop to school on a zebra.'

'Quite contradictory,' tutted Witch

Buggins. 'As you're moving on to Potions: Part Two, you'll be given the list of ingredients needed but the magic spells must now come from you. Your cauldron will do exactly what you ask it to do, so use your spell words wisely to avoid a cauldron catastrophe. And do take care to use the right ingredients and measure the quantities correctly. You don't want your Dream Dust exploding into fire-cracking, fizz-whizzing, sizzling sparkles. So, haste not waste, let's get brewing.'

The witches opened up their Witch Tablets on 'Potions: Part Two'. Grace-Ella worked next to Aisha and Twilight, with Mati and Moonbeam and Dilys and Dobbles at the other end of their table.

'What's your dreamiest dream?' Grace-Ella asked Aisha.

'It's to use my magic to help with medicines. Dad's a doctor and he's always telling me about illnesses around the world. I'm going to build my own laboratory and work day and night on my potions to cure illnesses.'

'Wow! That's an amazing dream,' said Grace-Ella. The only dream she could think of right then was that she could be as brilliantly brave and clever as Mati and Aisha.

Cork stoppers popped as potion bottles were opened and ingredients were poured, scooped and sprinkled into the cauldrons.

'Six sprigs of lavender and three pretty petals from the pink lady's slipper flower,' Grace-Ella said, as she measured the ingredients and Mr Whiskins plopped them into the cauldron. 'Seven spoonfuls of sticky, syrupy sap and a handful of sleepy grass. A ladle of lemon balm and a scrape of bark to add a small spark.'

'Once you've said your magic spell, the Dream Dust will shimmer on the surface,' said Witch Buggins, scuttling around the tables. 'Gently scoop it out with your strainers and pour it into the little silk pouches.'

Grace-Ella stirred her potion with her wooden spoon and said her magic words:

'Bubble and simmer sweet and bright,
My dreamiest dream I'll dream tonight.
Moonbeam light shine down on me,
A brave and brilliant witch I'll be.'

Her Dream Dust began to glimmer in a kaleidoscope of colours. She reached for her strainer to scoop out the dust, but it gave a jittering jump out of her hand and across the table. Her potion bottles rattled and her cauldron began to teeter.

'What's happening?' she whispered to Aisha, whose cauldron was also juddering and shuddering.

'I have no idea…'

They held on tightly to their cauldrons to stop their potions from sploshing onto the table.

Dilys stared in horror as her cauldron began to bubble and boil uncontrollably. A colourful cloud shot out. It crackled in the air then exploded with an almighty BANG! and showered the witches with Dream Dust.

'Bugs-and-grubs, this is bad. This is maggoty bad,' grumbled Witch Buggins, diving for shelter under a table.

One by one, the Dream-Dust-covered witches yawned loudly and dropped to the ground, their eyes drifting closed. Within seconds, the wooden gazebo was silent as the witches and their cats fell into a deep, dreamy sleep.

Chapter Nine
Bubble-Bounce

Grace-Ella's nose twitched. She opened her eyes and was surprised to see that she was still in the wooden gazebo.

'Bugs and grubs, thank buzzles it's working,' she heard Witch Buggins say. Brushing a peppery powder off her face, she stood up. Mr Whiskins stretched lazily at her feet. The other witches were slowly lifting themselves from the floor, bleary-eyed and bemused.

'What on earth happened?' asked Mati, her curly hair now a wild, tangled nest.

'It was all my fault,' whimpered Dilys.

'Now, now, now, mop up those tears,' said Witch Buggins, scooting over to their table. 'Blunders happen. No harm done. My Shake Awake powder has done the trick. We can't have a camp full of slumbering sloths, now can we?'

She handed Dilys a hankie to blow her nose, which once again startled Dobbles who leapt into the air and landed with a mighty meow on top of Mr Whiskins.

'I should explain,' said Dilys. 'It was all my fault because…'

'It was just a mistake,' interrupted Mati. 'We all make mistakes. She won't get punished, will she?'

'Bugs and grubs, no need for punishment.'

'But…' tried Dilys again.

'Mati's right,' said Grace-Ella. 'Mam's always making mistakes when she has to bake a cake. They usually end up like rocks. She always blames it on the oven.'

'But you don't understand,' said Dilys.

Before she could say any more, Witch Buggins climbed back onto her wooden step. 'Due to this unforeseen explosion, I'll have to postpone our Cauldron Class so that I can get the place cleaned up. I'd like you to gather your things and head back to your cabins for a shower. We'll meet around the campfire for tea.'

The witches showered and changed into fresh clothes. The witch cats also had to be lathered and brushed clean until their black coats were luminous. Dilys sat sadly on her bunk with Dobbles wrapped up in a towel on her lap.

'Don't be upset,' said Grace-Ella, sitting down next to her. 'Any of us could have added the wrong ingredient. I once stuck my mam to the kitchen ceiling with one of my potions!'

'It wasn't just a one-off mistake though,' whispered Dilys. 'It's because I…'

'It will all be forgotten about tomorrow,' said Aisha. 'You'll see.'

'And it won't go against us when it comes

to being the best coven, I'm sure of it,' added Mati.

'I shouldn't be here. I should get sent home,' sniffled Dilys. 'Then you'd have a much better chance of winning the Best Coven prize.'

'Don't be silly,' said Grace-Ella. 'It doesn't matter about being the best coven. We're your friends and we want you to stay. Come on, let's go to the campfire. You'll feel much better after some tea, that's what grown-ups always say.'

The campfire crackled cosily as the witches ate toasted cinnamon buns with fresh fruit skewers and drank lilac-coloured lavender lemonade.

'As our Cauldron Class went all to pot earlier, Penelope Pendle has instructed that

I should give you a Spelling Test instead,'
said Witch Buggins.

The witches groaned. A spelling test didn't
sound half as much fun as preparing potions.

'I'm useless at spelling tests,' worried
Grace-Ella. 'I can never remember my words
at school.'

'It's not that kind of spelling test,' said Mr
Whiskins. 'You're at Witch Camp, not St
Winifred's. This is a magic spells test.'

'Oh, of course,' said Grace-Ella. 'I think the
Dream Dust has left my brain a bit snoozy.'

With their notebooks on their laps, the
witches wrote down the answers to Witch
Buggins's spelling questions.

'Which of these magic spells would you
use to cheer someone up if they were feeling
unwell? Teardrop Stop, Tickle Pickle or
Giggles and Wiggles?'

Grace-Ella wasn't sure. They all sounded like cheer-up spells.

'Which answer would you choose?' she whispered to Mr Whiskins.

'Let's work through it together. If you were ill right now, would you want anyone tickling you? Would you be likely to be crying? Or would you just want someone to make you laugh?'

'Hmm… Well, I don't like being tickled at any time and I usually just feel miserable when I'm unwell… Mr Whiskins, you're the brightest and best witch cat in the world,' said Grace-Ella, writing down 'Giggles and Wiggles'.

As Witch Buggins asked more questions, the young witches began to yawn, their eyes drooped and their heads nodded heavily.

'Bugs and grubs, this won't do,' said Witch

Buggins. 'You're all still sleepy. The Dream Dust clearly hasn't worn off properly. Notebooks down, I know just how to wake things up around here.'

She began to prepare a potion in her cauldron.

'A grasshopper's hop and a spider web's sheen,
The ribbit of a frog and a jellied bean.
Slivers of soap and five drops of dew,
A sticky snail trail and a dollop of glue.'

She mixed it all up and said the magic words.

'Bubble-Bounce hop and bop,
Twist and twirl like a spinning top,
Up sky-high then down you'll drop,
Bubble-Bounce before you pop!'

Out of the cauldron floated ginormous bubbles. The young witches were suddenly wide awake as they watched the bubbles bob above them.

'Stand up for the fun,' said Witch Buggins, her eyes twinkling with mischief. The bubbles floated down onto the witches and their cats until they were standing right inside them!

'Bubble-Bounce!' shouted Witch Buggins, waving her magic wand.

The bubbles bounced. They bounced up high, spinning and twirling in the dusky sky. The young witches whooped and squealed as they tumbled about inside their bubbles. They bounced until they were all wibbly-wobbly on their feet and their faces were rosy-bright. Even Dilys was laughing loudly.

'I think that's quite enough.'

Penelope Pendle's voice pierced the evening air. The witches didn't want their Bubble-Bounce fun to end, but Penelope Pendle was looking very stern.

'Down they come, please, Witch Buggins.' Witch Buggins waved her wand and the bubbles floated down to the ground and popped.

'I can see that you've had a lot of fun with Witch Buggins,' said Penelope Pendle, 'but you have another busy day tomorrow. After today's potion commotion, I think you should head to your cabins for an early night. You can work on your Potion Test before settling down for a good night's sleep.'

'Rats,' muttered Mati, as she answered a second potion question incorrectly and missed out on another gold star. 'My brain is too sleepy for this. I'm going to pause it and finish first thing in the morning.'

Everyone agreed to do the same. They were all exhausted and ready to burrow in their bunks.

'Tomorrow it's Broomsticks with Witch Willow,' said Aisha, who always remembered to check their timetable at bedtime.

'Brill,' uttered Mati, far too tired for once for any more words.

Chapter 10
Broomsticks

'A witch's feet are slightly outward pointing to help keep a firm grip on our broomstick. The technical term is the "Heel-Squeeze", explained Witch Willow.

Witch Willow was like an owl. She was full of facts and had enormous, round, golden eyes, which caught every little movement. No one talked when Witch Willow was speaking. She would swoop and be standing in front of you before you could snap your mouth shut.

'We'll be heading to Whispering Willow Woods to gather the willow leaves needed for our broomsticks. And then this evening we'll have the Broomstick Bonanza where you'll learn how to fly.'

'This is more exciting than Christmas,' gasped Grace-Ella.

The broomstick excitement was contagious. It spread from one witch to the next like fire-lit string.

At the edge of Whispering Willow Woods, the willow trees bowed and their branches formed an archway.

'Willow trees grow close to wetland and the ground can be very marshy. The path is overgrown, but we should be able to follow it to the weeping willow tree. The magical leaves from this tree are the only ones we can use as twine for our broomsticks. Without this magical twine, your broomstick will do no more than sweep your cabin floor.'

Dappled sunlight shone through the

canopy of tall trees and danced on the woodland path.

Witch Willow eventually stopped at the bottom of steep stone steps that seemed to climb to the clouds. 'These are the hundred stone steps that lead to the weeping willow.'

They were all breathless by the time they climbed to the top. The trees were sparse, creating a clearing circled by large moss-green rocks. In the middle stood the weeping willow. An eerie mist hovered over the tree's branches. Its trunk was thick and knobbly.

'Approach the tree quietly,' whispered Witch Willow. 'You each need to collect ten leaves for your twine.'

The girls tiptoed to the tree, the ground spongy-wet underfoot. The mist felt like weepy tears on their cheeks. They each plucked ten of the long, drooping leaves from the branches.

'Well done, witches. Now let's go back to camp to make our broomsticks.'

Back at the Glade, the witches once again gathered under the wooden gazebo. On the tables were long broom handles made of ash wood, which Aisha explained to her friends was the best wood to use for balance.

'Use the handsaws to cut the birch twigs for your broomstick's bristles. Try to cut them into equal lengths.'

The witches snapped and sawed their twigs. Witch Willow demonstrated how to tie a Witch's Knot. Once they could confidently tie the knot with string, they used a Witch's Knot to tie the bristles to the handle with their willow leaves.

'So you can always recognise your own broom, you can carve your choice of patterns onto the handle.'

The afternoon flew by as the witches whittled patterns onto their broom handles. As the sky began to darken, their broomsticks were ready for the Bonanza.

'Broomsticks can be bothersome,' warned Witch Willow. 'You need to grip tightly with both your hands and feet. The Broomsticks for Beginners magic spell is written on the tag tied at the top of the handle. Keep the broomstick steady as you say the magic words. Slowly raise the handle upwards. Don't point it too high or too low. To speed up, lean forward, to slow down, lean back. Shift to the left or right to change direction. Now I want you to spread out in your groups so that we avoid any bashes and crashes. Once you're feeling steady and ready, hold on tight and say the magic words.'

The young witches spread out around the Glade, making sure that they had plenty of clear space.

Grace-Ella grasped her broomstick and read the magic words:

"Broomstick, broomstick, now take flight,
Up into this starry night.
Fly up high and swoop down low,
With willow magic off we go.'

She pointed her broom handle upwards and slowly felt her feet leave the ground. As she rose higher, she wobbled a little, and her broomstick swayed beneath her.

'Come on,' squealed Mati, who was far too adventurous to stay hovering near the

ground. She sped forwards, made a sharp turn and zoomed back to Grace-Ella, Aisha and Dilys (who still had her feet firmly on the ground).

Feeling steadier now that she had found her balance, Grace-Ella sped up a little. The air blew through her hair and whistled in her ears.

'I never truly believed I would learn to fly on a broomstick,' said Grace-Ella, her eyes sparkling.

'It's the best fun ever,' replied Mati, risking a daring loop-the-loop. 'Come on, Dilys. Don't be scared. It's broomstick-brilliant.'

As they dipped and dived, propelled and slowed, something suddenly whooshed past, making them spin full circle.

'It's Dilys!' shouted Mati. 'And it looks like she's got herself into a bit of broomstick bother.'

Mati leaned forward and raced after her. Grace-Ella pointed her broomstick downwards and landed with a thud on the ground. She ran over to Witch Willow and panted, breathless, 'Dilys. Her broomstick. Too fast. Heading for *Fir Tree Forest*.'

At that very moment, they all heard a calamitous crash. 'It sounds like she's landed,' said Witch Willow, leaping onto her broomstick and zipping towards the forest.

Mati and Aisha landed safely and rushed over to Grace-Ella.

'Dobbles clambered onto her head,' explained Mati. 'His tail was swishing in front of her eyes like windscreen wipers. She couldn't see where she was going or what she was doing.'

A few minutes later, Witch Willow returned with Dilys and Dobbles on the back of her broomstick. Dilys had scratches on her face from the tree branches and a black bruise blooming around her left eye.

'You're lucky you're not as broken as your broomstick,' said Witch Willow. 'Didn't I say slow and steady? And what magic words did you use for your broomstick to behave so disobediently? You were instructed to read the Broomsticks for Beginners spell.'

'I did… I mean, I tried… It's just that I couldn't…'

'I don't want to hear any excuses, Dilys Dibble,' said Witch Willow. 'Broomsticks are not allowed to whoosh about in such a reckless manner. A lesson has hopefully been learnt.' She handed Dilys a bottle of ointment. 'Rub this into your scratches and bruises and get yourself off to bed.'

The other three returned to the cabin with Dilys.

'What happened?' asked Aisha.

'It's just me,' said Dilys. 'I'm a useless witch. I can't get anything right.'

'You're not useless,' said Aisha. 'I think you're just unlucky.'

'No, I need…'

'No, you don't need to be sent home,' interrupted Grace-Ella.

'They're right,' said Mati. 'We just need to come up with a plan to help you.'

'I have the perfect plan,' said Aisha, smiling widely. 'We'll help you to fix your broomstick and teach you how to fly it properly.'

'My broomstick was so badly broken, Witch Willow said it would be used as firewood.'

'Well then we'll help you make you a brand new broomstick,' said Aisha.

'Brilliant,' said Mati.

'But we don't have any willow leaves left,' said Grace-Ella.

'No, we don't,' agreed Aisha. 'But we know where to get them from.'

'You mean go back to Whispering Willow Woods?' asked Grace-Ella.

'Mmm-hmm…'

'Broomsticky brilliant,' said Mati.

'You're all so kind, I feel dreadful,' said Dilys. 'You don't need to help me make a new broomstick. You can't miss tomorrow's Sparkling Spells. Penelope Pendle told us that we're not to miss any of the activities.'

'Who said anything about waiting until tomorrow?' said Aisha. 'After cabin lights-out, we'll go back to the woods. There are spare handles and bristles in the gazebo. We'll have a new broomstick ready for you before the sun comes up.'

'But we can't go out after cabin lights-out,' said Dilys with a shiver. 'We'll get into trouble.'

'And the woods will be dark. We won't be able to find our way,' said Grace-Ella, feeling nervous about going out into the dark night.

'We'll take our fireflies,' said Aisha.

'They'll light the way for us.'

'But if we get caught…' uttered Grace-Ella.

'We won't. We'll be extra careful. And we have to help Dilys. This is the only way.'

The four witches looked at each other. Grace-Ella felt a flicker of fear, but as long as she was with her witch friends, she was sure everything would work out fine.

'So, are we all in?' asked Aisha.

'We're a coven, and covens stick together,' said Mati. 'Let's do it.'

Chapter 11
The Belching Bog

The four friends dressed in their darkest clothes and crept as quiet as church mice through the camp. Everyone agreed that Dobbles should stay behind and rest after his earlier fright. Dilys wrapped him up in his blanket with his favourite soft mouse tucked between his front paws, and soothed him to sleep.

The moon played hide-and-seek behind the clouds. Bats fluttered over their heads and an owl hooted. The tall trees of Whispering Willow Woods were now shadowy silhouettes. Leaves rustled and night-time creatures scurried to hide in the undergrowth. Mr Whiskins couldn't help

chasing after them.

'It looks so different in the dark,' said
Grace-Ella. 'What if we can't find the
stone steps?'

'The fireflies will lead the way,'
answered Aisha.

A movement caught Grace-Ella's eye.
Another small glowing light was flittering
through the trees. 'What's that?' she said.

'Maybe it's another firefly?' said Mati. 'I bet it's Cabin Six. Didn't I say they looked like they were plotting something. I knew it.'

'It's too big to be a firefly … and besides there's more than four … lots more,' said Aisha.

Dozens of golden dots flickered in the woods. A soft whispering breeze blew against their faces like the swish of a feather.

'I think they're willow fairies,' exclaimed Aisha. 'I've read about them. They live in willow trees and come out at night.'

'They must have come out to help us,' said Mati.

'I don't think so,' said Aisha. 'I read that they try to lead travellers astray.'

'Frogspawn! Fairies are friendly, everyone knows that,' said Mati. 'I think they're showing us the way to the stone steps.'

With their fireflies fluttering overhead, they

followed the dancing golden globes through the trees. The ground became very wet.

'I don't think we're going the right way,' said Grace-Ella. 'The ground wasn't this boggy earlier.'

'The ground always gets damper at night. I'm sure we'll see the stone steps any second,' said Mati.

The fairies darted in and out of the trees. Mati and Moonbeam jumped over fallen branches, hurrying to keep up with them. Aisha tried to keep up with Mati, Twilight right by her side.

'Something doesn't feel right,' said Grace-Ella, slowing down when her shoes began to squelch in the mud. 'I've got a funny feeling in my tummy.'

Just then, Mr Whiskins bounded out of the trees with worried whiskers. 'Don't go any further. Aisha was right. The willow fairies are leading you away from the path and straight towards the Belching Bog.'

'On no!' cried Grace-Ella and Dilys. 'Stop!' they shouted, but there was no answer. There was no sign of Mati and Aisha.

The golden lights headed back towards them. Whispered words floated in the night sky. 'This way, this way, follow me. I'll lead you to the willow tree.'

'Don't listen to them,' said Mr Whiskins. 'They're trying to trick you.'

'We have to stop Mati and Aisha before they end up in the Belching Bog,' said Grace-Ella, with a tremble in her voice.

They quickly retraced their steps until they were safely back on the path. They ran along it, shouting out their friends' names.

'Aisha? Mati? Where are you?'

Grace-Ella wished they hadn't dressed in dark clothes. They had thought it would help them to sneak unnoticed through the campsite. Now she wished her friends were wearing the brightest, shiniest colours. They were beginning to lose hope when they heard a voice.

'Help! We're stuck in the Belching Bog.'

'It's Mati,' shouted Grace-Ella. 'Come on. We'll have to risk leaving the path.'

'I have an excellent sense of smell,' said Mr Whiskins. 'I'll smell the bog's belches first, so I'll go in front.'

They left the path, following the faint glow of their fireflies. Mr Whiskins stopped, his snout in the air. 'I smell a whiffy pong. We're nearly there.'

'Help! Please help!' It was Mati again.

This time her voice sounded much closer.

'We're coming,' shouted Grace-Ella.

They ducked under branches and stumbled over exposed roots. The ground was getting soggier. The air smelt rancid. When they could hear a loud belching noise, they skidded to a stop.

Just a few steps ahead bubbled the Belching Bog. It looked like an enormous bowl of greeny-brown gloop. Large bubbles burst on the surface with a stink.

Right in the middle stood Mati and Aisha, waist-deep in the foul-smelling sludge. With each putrid bubble, they sank a tiny bit deeper. Moonbeam and Twilight had luckily managed to clamber onto an overhanging branch.

'Don't worry, we'll get you out,' said Grace-Ella, even though she had no idea how.

'What are we going to do?' whispered Dilys.

'We'll find some long branches and pull them out,' said Grace-Ella, trying her best to stay calm and confident even though she felt like a great big wibbly jelly.

'It's no use, Moonbeam and Twilight tried pulling us out with tree vines. This disgusting stuff is like the stickiest superglue ever,' said Mati.

'There's an ancient spell that can stop the belching. I read about it in Witch Studies,' shouted Aisha. 'That's the only way out of the bog.'

'But we don't know the ancient spell,' said Grace-Ella. 'We'll have to go back to camp. Penelope Pendle will know what to do.'

'You can't go back to camp. We'll be in so much trouble. We'll have our magic taken

from us,' said Mati. 'I am *not* going to let
that happen.'

'Mati's right,' said Aisha. 'We're born to
be witches and if we have our magic taken
from us, then we'll no longer be allowed to
keep our cats...'

Grace-Ella fought back tears. Her heart
would shatter into a trillion pieces if she

lost Mr Whiskins. 'But we can't just stand here and watch you disappear!'

'Aunty Lilith says I must always be brave in the face of danger,' said Mati, raising her chin defiantly. 'Witch Hazel was right. We are going to end up d-e-a-d. I want you to know that you're the bestest witch friends that I could ever have had.'

'You're not going to let a belching bog beat you, are you?' called Aisha. 'Where's your bravery and confidence that made you loop-the-loop on your broomstick and grab onto the stinging screamer?'

'That's it! The stinging screamer!' yowled Mr Whiskins. 'That's where we'll get the ancient spell from.'

'But we don't have a stinging screamer,' said Grace-Ella.

'Not yet you don't,' said Aisha. 'But you

can get one. I know you can.'

'Genius,' said Mati. 'I should have thought of that. I definitely need to do more studying if I get out of this stinking situation alive.'

'You have to go back to Fir Tree Forest and pull up the stinging screamer,' called Aisha.

'There has to be another way. I'll never be able to do it,' said Grace-Ella, overwhelmed that everyone was looking to her. There was no way that she could sort this sticky, sinking mess out by herself. She hadn't won all her gold stars in her tests. She wasn't clever like Aisha or brave like Mati.

'Yes, you will,' said Mr Whiskins. 'You're a magnifulous-splendifulous witch.'

'It's their only chance,' said Dilys. 'I'll stay here and keep watch so that I know where they are in case … in case they disappear before you get back.'

Grace-Ella looked at Aisha and Mati sinking slowly in the Belching Bog. She looked at Mr Whiskins, whose green eyes were shining with determination. It really was up to her.

'OK, I'll try my very best, I promise.'

With a final glance at their friends, Grace-Ella and Mr Whiskins headed back into the woods.

Chapter 12
The Daring Scaring Rescue

Grace-Ella and Mr Whiskins staggered out of Whispering Willow Woods. They ran towards Fir Tree Forest.

'The middle of the forest felt frightening earlier,' said Grace-Ella. 'And I'll never be able to pull up the stinging screamer. Mati couldn't even do it and she's a much better witch than me.'

'Being brave doesn't mean that she's better than you,' said Mr Whiskins. 'You can only try your best, but I have furry faith that you can do this.'

It didn't take them long to reach the dark belly of the forest. It was still and silent. The moon had disappeared behind thick clouds. Grace-Ella's firefly landed on the fallen tree that hid the screamer.

'You can do this,' said Mr Whiskins. 'You're the most magnifulous-splendifulous witch in the whole world … which is why I was chosen as your cat, of course. We make the purrrfect team.'

Swallowing as much of her panic as she could, deep down into her belly, Grace-Ella placed her trembling hands around the stinging screamer's stalk. Her heart thud-thudded and despite the cold night air, sweat tickled her brow. She took in one long, deep breath and began to pull.

The screaming started and she instantly let go. 'See! I can't do it,' she cried.

'Harness your magic powers, that's what Witch Hazel said,' said Mr Whiskins.

'But I don't know how to harness my magic.

I don't even know what harness means.'

'Close your eyes and think of all the magical things that have happened since you've become a witch,' said Mr Whiskins.

Grace-Ella once again placed her hands around the stinging screamer. This time when she started to pull, she closed her eyes and thought of all the good things that becoming a witch had brought her.

She thought about her best friends at home, Fflur and Bedwyr, and their excitement when she had revealed her secret to them. She thought of how her magic had helped her to teach Amelia, the school bully, a lesson. She thought of her new friends at Witch Camp. And most of all, she thought of her precious Mr Whiskins, the best cat anyone could wish for.

She opened her eyes.

'You did it,' purred Mr Whiskins proudly.

Grace-Ella looked down. Dangling from her hands was the stinging screamer. She had done it! She had pulled up the most magical plant of all.

'I think I'm in a dream and I'll wake up safe and sound in my bunk,' she said, then gasped. 'Look! The flowers are closing up. I think it's dying. The spell will be lost. What

am I going to do?'

'Maybe it should be in a pot and fed straight away,' said Mr Whiskins.

'But we haven't got a pot,' cried Grace-Ella, looking about in the hope that a pot would magically appear before her. 'I'll have to plant it back in the ground.'

They dug up a pile of fresh damp soil and replanted the stinging screamer. Grace-Ella watched as its roots uncurled and burrowed deep. Slowly, the cream flowers opened up.

'It worked,' she said, relief crashing over her like an ocean wave. 'Let's hope it will still reveal the ancient spell.'

She grabbed her notebook from her backpack and crouched on the ground.

'Stinging screamer, please help me to stop the Belching Bog from swallowing my friends.'

One of the flowers twizzled on its stalk to face Grace-Ella. She pressed her ear next to the fuzzy petals and wrote down everything she heard.

'Murky bog with your belching stink,
Still your surface, bubbles sink.
Hold your breath in way down deep,
This starry night you'll fall asleep.'

Grace-Ella beamed with pride. 'I've got the magic spell. I can save Aisha and Mati … if I'm not too late.' She tore the page from her notebook. 'Come on, let's go.'

Grace-Ella and Mr Whiskins headed back once more to Whispering Willow Woods.

Chapter 13
Mystery Solved

It was much easier to find the Belching Bog this time.

'I've got the ancient spell,' shouted Grace-Ella, as she tore through the trees.

She stared in horror at the bog. Aisha had sunk so deep that she was straining to keep her chin out of the bubbling depths. Mati, who was the tallest, had sunk up to her shoulders.

'I knew you could do it,' said Aisha.

The bog belched once more and dragged the two witches further down. There was no time to waste. Grace-Ella climbed the tree with the overhanging branch as quickly as a cat. She stretched herself flat and threw the tree vines out to the middle of the bog.

'Hold on to the vines. I don't know how long it will take for the spell to work.'

With one hand grasping the vines, she rummaged in her pocket with the other and pulled out the ancient spell.

A gust of wind whipped the paper from her hand and sent it spinning away from her.

'Grab it!' she shouted to Dilys.

The bog bubbled and let out another belch. Mati's shoulders disappeared. Aisha gave a short scream as she sank again.

'Read the spell!' shrieked Grace-Ella.

Quaking to her bones, Dilys picked up the sheet of paper. 'I can't.'

'Of course you can,' shouted Aisha. 'Hurry. Read the spell! I think I'll disappear with the next belch.'

'I can't,' repeated Dilys.

'Just read it!' screamed Mati.

And at that moment, Grace-Ella understood. All the puzzle pieces fell into a picture. Why had it taken her so long to see what had been right under her nose the whole time?

Before Grace-Ella could say anything, the bog bubbled and belched. Was Aisha going to disappear? Twilight howled like a wild wolf. His cry echoed high in the Black Mountains.

'You beastly bog,' screamed Mati. She tried to reach out to Aisha but it was no use. Her whole body was stuck firm.

Grace-Ella shouted, 'Mr Whiskins, you have to bring me the spell! NOW!'

Like a flash of lightning, Mr Whiskins leapt into action. He snatched the paper

from Dilys and scrambled up the tree. He
pushed the magic spell into Grace-Ella's hand.

Wiping her eyes with her sleeve, Grace-Ella
read aloud the ancient spell.

'Murky bog with your belching stink,
Still your surface, bubbles sink.
Hold your breath in way down deep,
This starry night you'll fall asleep.'

They waited. The woodland was silent. The Belching Bog was still.

'It's working,' shouted Mati suddenly, pulling her arms unstuck.

The surface of the bog rippled, and like an erupting volcano, Aisha jumped up, gasping and spluttering.

Mati and Aisha held hands and pushed their way to the bank. They climbed out, boggy sludge dripping from them. Grace-Ella and Dilys lunged forward and wrapped their arms around them. Moonbeam and Twilight rubbed against their legs.

'Now we're all a stinking mess,' laughed Aisha.

'Who cares?' said Grace-Ella, hugging her friends tighter.

Exhausted, they sat on the bank of the Belching Bog. Mati and Aisha's muscles ached from fighting against the strong undercurrent that had tried to pull them into the bog forever.

But then Mati frowned.

Dilys looked nervous.

'Dilys!' screeched Mati. 'Why didn't you read the spell? We could have ended up dead!'

'She couldn't,' Grace-Ella jumped in, looking at Dilys, who started crying and hid her head in her hands.

'What do you mean she couldn't?' Mati demanded.

'Dilys can't read … can you?' said Grace-Ella. 'Everything makes sense now. Your potion labels, the Dream Dust explosion, your out-of-control broomstick … and Bella Bwt, of course. Why didn't I see what The Book of Rules was trying to tell me? You're just like Bella. She couldn't read either.'

'Who's Bella?' asked Mati. 'And everyone can read.'

'No, they can't,' said Aisha. 'Think of the children in countries who don't have a school to go to. They can't read because they've never been given the chance to learn.'

'But Dilys goes to school like the rest of us,' replied Mati.

'No, I don't,' said Dilys.

Dilys explained that her family decided she would be taught witch lessons at home by her mam-gu. From the day she was born, they knew she was a witch and they wanted her to be the best witch ever. In their excitement, they forgot that she needed to learn normal things as well.

'I memorise the spells that Mam-gu

reads out to me and then I can repeat them,' explained Dilys. 'But it's hard to remember every detail, which is why my spells and potions never quite work.'

'Haven't you told your mam and dad that you can't read?' asked Grace-Ella.

'I didn't want to upset them. They're completely obsessed with making me a magnificent witch. I think my magic has blinded them.'

'Oh, Dilys,' said Grace-Ella, putting her arm around her friend's shoulders.

'Why didn't you tell us straight away?' asked Aisha. 'We would have helped you.'

'I was too embarrassed. I thought you wouldn't want me in your coven, but I really liked you all and I wanted to stay with you. And when things started to go wrong, I tried to tell you, but the words never seemed to come out of my mouth.'

'You don't need to be embarrassed,' said Grace-Ella. 'And we would never have wanted you to leave our coven. Covens stick together, remember.'

'Absolutely right,' said Mati. 'We are the Midnight Roses and nothing is ever going to change that. All we need to do is cast a reading spell on you.'

'We can't cast a spell on her. Rule 7: Never cast a spell on another witch,' said Aisha.

'Rats! You're right. You really do know your witch stuff,' said Mati.

The sky was beginning to get lighter and the birds in the woods started to chirrup their morning chorus.

'We'd better get back to camp before the others wake up,' said Grace-Ella. 'After everything we've been through, we don't want to fall at the final hurdle.'

'But we never got the willow leaves to make you a new broomstick,' said Mati.

'I don't care about having a broomstick,' said Dilys. 'I have everything I need right here. The best friends in the whole world.'

Chapter 14
The Midnight Roses

Camp was quiet. They sneaked past the glowing embers of the campfire towards their cabin.

'We've got away with it,' whispered Aisha. 'No one will ever know…'

They stopped. Standing in front of their cabin door was Penelope Pendle. Her eyebrows were raised. Her foot was tapping.

'Good morning,' she said. 'Up a little early today, aren't you?'

The four friends stared at the ground. Grace-Ella felt a prickly feeling spread up her neck to her face, like an army of ants scurrying over her.

'Umm … yes,' said Aisha. 'We … umm … thought we'd enjoy a morning stroll. Fresh air. Nothing better.'

'Really,' said Penelope Pendle, her eyebrows now so high they were about to hover above her head.

Dilys looked up. 'It's OK. You don't have to lie. This is all my fault. I'll explain everything and then you can send me home, but please don't punish the others. All they've done is try to help me.'

'If we're going to sit down for a little talk, I think it's best you shower and change first,' said Penelope Pendle. 'The early morning air may be fresh, but you four most certainly aren't.'

After they were cleaned up and the cats were fast asleep, Penelope Pendle led the four friends to her cabin, where there were four mugs of sweet tea waiting for them.

'So,' said Penelope Pendle, 'who's going to start?'

She sat still and listened whilst the four girls explained everything.

'I'm so sorry that we broke your rules,'

said Dilys. 'I should have told the truth as soon as I arrived, then none of this would have happened.'

'Well, telling the truth would certainly have saved you a lot of worry,' said Penelope Pendle, 'but I can understand why you felt unable to.'

'We really only wanted to help,' said Mati. 'And it isn't Dilys's fault. She shouldn't be punished just because she can't read.'

'I can see that you've become very close friends and it was very kind, if a little irresponsible, to try to help Dilys,' said Penelope Pendle.

'Are we going to get sent home?' asked Grace-Ella, imagining her mother's disappointment.

Penelope Pendle looked at the four young witches sitting before her.

'I think you've had a very frightening experience,' she said, 'which is punishment enough. You should have come to me instead of wandering off alone in the middle of the night. I can see that you felt it was an emergency. I did say you were not to leave your cabins after lights-out, *unless* it was for an emergency.'

'Does that mean we get to stay?' asked Aisha. 'Do we get to finish our activities and come to the Leaving Ceremony tomorrow morning?'

'Yes, you can all stay. I'm very proud of the way you pulled together to help each other. It was very courageous of you.' She turned to Grace-Ella. 'And you pulled up the stinging screamer?'

'Umm … yes,' said Grace-Ella.

'That's really rather astonishing,' said

Penelope Pendle. 'I think you must be the youngest witch to achieve this.'

Grace-Ella blushed beetroot-red.

Penelope Pendle smiled. 'Go on, go and join the others for breakfast. You must be starving after your night-time adventure.'

During breakfast, everyone wanted to talk to Grace-Ella about the stinging screamer.

'You're going to be famous,' said Mati. 'Famous people have assistants to help them and I'm more than happy to be your assistant, if no one else wants to, that is.'

'That's very kind of you, Mati,' said Grace-Ella laughing, 'but the only assistant I'll ever need is Mr Whiskins.'

That day's activity was Sparkling Spells with Witch Wanda. Dilys was asked to spend the day with Penelope Pendle. They didn't see her until they were sitting around the campfire for supper.

'So what happened?' asked Grace-Ella.

'She was really wonderful. She's going to talk to Mam-gu and Mam and Dad and explain everything. Witch Wanda is going to be my very own witch tutor.'

'That's fantastic news,' said Grace-Ella.

'I can't wait,' said Dilys. 'And Penelope Pendle thinks that Dobbles is so afraid of everything because he's been so worried about me all this time. She said that now I'm happy and can become a proper witch, his confidence will grow too. And Witch Catkins is going to be calling by to help him.'

Grace-Ella, Mati and Aisha were thrilled for their friend. Everything had worked out brilliantly.

'Well, your first Witch Camp has come to an end,' said Penelope Pendle on Friday morning.

The young witches were dressed in their new black cloaks.

'I hope you've all enjoyed your week and have lots of new magic to take home with you. You've all worked very hard and have tried your best and I'm extremely proud of you all. To earn your Spells for Beginners certificate, you needed to win at least eighty gold stars out of the possible one hundred. So let's not waste any more time. Let's reveal the scores.'

A holographic score board appeared at the front of the gazebo. The young witches waited anxiously to see if their names would appear.

'Our Witch of the Week who has won the

most stars is … Aisha Patel.'

Grace-Ella, Mati and Dilys squealed in delight. The other witches clapped their hands. Aisha's name appeared at the top of the leader board and a gold star with the number ninety-five flashed beside it.

'Come to the front to collect your certificate and your Witch of the Week badge.'

One by one, the names of the witches appeared on the board with the number of stars they had won next to their names. As more and more names appeared, Grace-Ella began to have a sinking feeling that she hadn't passed.

Mati's name appeared with a score of eighty-five in her gold star.

Grace-Ella crossed her fingers and tried once again to cross her toes as she waited to see her score in her gold star…

Finally her name appeared. Eighty-two. She had passed! She felt like she was floating as she skipped to the front to collect her Spells for Beginners certificate. Only four witches hadn't earned enough stars to pass. One of them was Dilys.

'For those of you who haven't passed, please don't feel disheartened. You just need a little more time to work on your *Spells for Beginners* and *Potions: Part One*. You'll have your certificates in no time at all. Now before you go to your cabins to pack your bags and prepare to leave, I have three more awards to give.'

The witches looked around, wondering what they were.

'The first special award is for the group of witches who have been the best coven this week. Being a coven means being a team

– helping and supporting each other. This week's award for Best Coven goes to … Cabin Number Two: Mati, Aisha, Dilys and Grace-Ella.'

The four witch friends linked arms and proudly walked to the front to collect their award.

'Didn't I tell you we'd be the best?' said Mati, pinning her Best Coven badge onto her cloak.

'Now if you'll stay at the front for a moment please,' said Penelope Pendle. 'My second special award is for a young witch who has achieved something incredible this week. My Super Star award goes to Grace-Ella for being the youngest witch ever to pull up the stinging screamer.'

The gazebo erupted into applause. The witches banged the tables and stomped their feet. Penelope Pendle handed Grace-Ella a golden star trophy with her name across the centre and a purple plant pot with glittery green stars around the rim, so she had a proper pot for her precious new plant.

'Your stinging screamer belongs to you now,' she said. 'I'll return to the forest with you when we're ready to leave so that you can collect it.'

Grace-Ella had never felt happier. 'I'm

going to call my plant Seren. She's far too beautiful and precious to be called a stinging screamer.'

'And of course, we mustn't forget about our faithful felines,' said Penelope Pendle. 'The Top Cat award goes to Mr Whiskins for his bravery and his belief in his witch, Grace-Ella.'

Mr Whiskins sauntered to the front and sat proudly at Grace-Ella's feet as Penelope Pendle tied a new purple collar with shiny golden stars around his neck.

'You're the best cat in the entire universe,' said Grace-Ella.

'And you are a magnifulous-splendifulous witch,' he purred.

All too soon it was time to head home. Grace-Ella placed her magic wand in her rucksack and carefully put her rolled-up Spells for Beginners certificate in her cloak pocket. She had learnt so much at Witch Camp and couldn't wait to share her witchy adventures with her parents and best friends.

She looked down at the special badges on her cloak. Not only was she leaving Witch Camp with a new broomstick and Seren, her stinging screamer plant, she was also leaving with three new friends and a little bit more magical confidence. Maybe Mr Whiskins was right. Maybe she was going to be a magnifulous-splendifulous witch. It seemed she hadn't needed her Dream Dust after all.

'I'm going to miss you all so much,' said Dilys as they headed out of the cabin.

'You'll be far too busy catching up with all your learning. You won't have time to miss us,' said Aisha. 'And we can keep in touch all the time to share all our witch news.'

'Definitely,' said Mati. 'We're the best coven ever and nothing is going to change that.'

'We're the Midnight Roses,' said Grace-Ella, 'forever.'

To find out how Grace-Ella first met Mr Whiskins
and became a witch, don't miss:

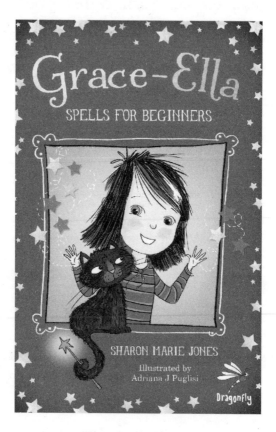

Grace-Ella: Spells for Beginners
9781910080429
find out more at *www.fireflypress.co.uk*